EAT noodles on TUESDAYS

BY **Jon Stahl**

ILLUSTRATED BY

Tadgh Bentley

SCHOLASTIC PRESS **NEW YORK**

For Sophie and Charlie,
the best characters
I've ever created.
And for Wendy.
—J.S.

To Freddie and Albie,
from Conkig.

—T.B.

• LIBRARY OF CONGRESS CATALOGING-IN-PUBLICATION DATA •

Names: Stahl, Jon, author. | Bentley, Tadgh, illustrator. • Title: Dragons eat noodles on Tuesdays / by Jon Stahl ; illustrated by Tadgh Bentley. • Description: First edition. | New York : Scholastic Press, 2019. | Summary: While two monsters argue over how the story they are telling should go, Dennis, a very hungry dragon, is listening nearby—and he has very definite ideas about how this story should end. • Identifiers: LCCN 2018002091 | ISBN 9781338125511 • Subjects: LCSH: Dragons—Juvenile fiction. | Monsters—Juvenile fiction. | Storytelling—Juvenile fiction. | Humorous stories. | CYAC: Dragons—Fiction. | Monsters—Fiction. | Storytelling—Fiction. | Humorous stories. | LCGFT: Humorous fiction. | Picture books. • Classification: LCC PZ7.1.S725 Dr 2019 | DDC [E]—dc23 LC record available at https://lccn.loc.gov/2018002091 • 10 9 8 7 6 5 4 3 2 1   19 20 21 22 23

• PRINTED IN CHINA   38 • FIRST EDITION, APRIL 2019 •

Tadgh Bentley's drawings were created using pencil and pen and were colored with digital gouache and watercolor brushes. The text type was set in KG Dancing on the Roof Regular. • The display type was set in KG King Cool KC Regular and Tw Cen MT Bold. The book was printed on 128gsm Golden Sun Matte and bound at RR Donnelley Asia. • Production was overseen by Angie Chen. Manufacturing was supervised by Shannon Rice. • The book was art directed and designed by Marijka Kostiw, and edited by Dianne Hess.

Maybe the dragon doesn't eat the kid. Maybe they are friends and go on cool adventures! There. That's nice.

Nice? Nice is boring. No, the dragon definitely needs to eat someone.

How about a story without a dragon?

Like what?

Like this:

Boy finds toy.

Boy loses toy.

Toy meets girl.

Girl loves toy.

Toy is happy.

Boy gets new toy.

I don't know.

Please, call me Dennis.
Put me down!
I don't care what they call you. You put that knight down, now!
Come on, I'm starving!

But the damsel was not only brave, she was also very smart.
Look, Dennis, everyone knows dragons ONLY eat noodles on Tuesdays!
ye olde dragon menu
monday
knights
tuesday
noodles (only)
wednesday
monsters
thursday
villagers
friday
king buffet
saturday
damsel dinner
sunday
salad

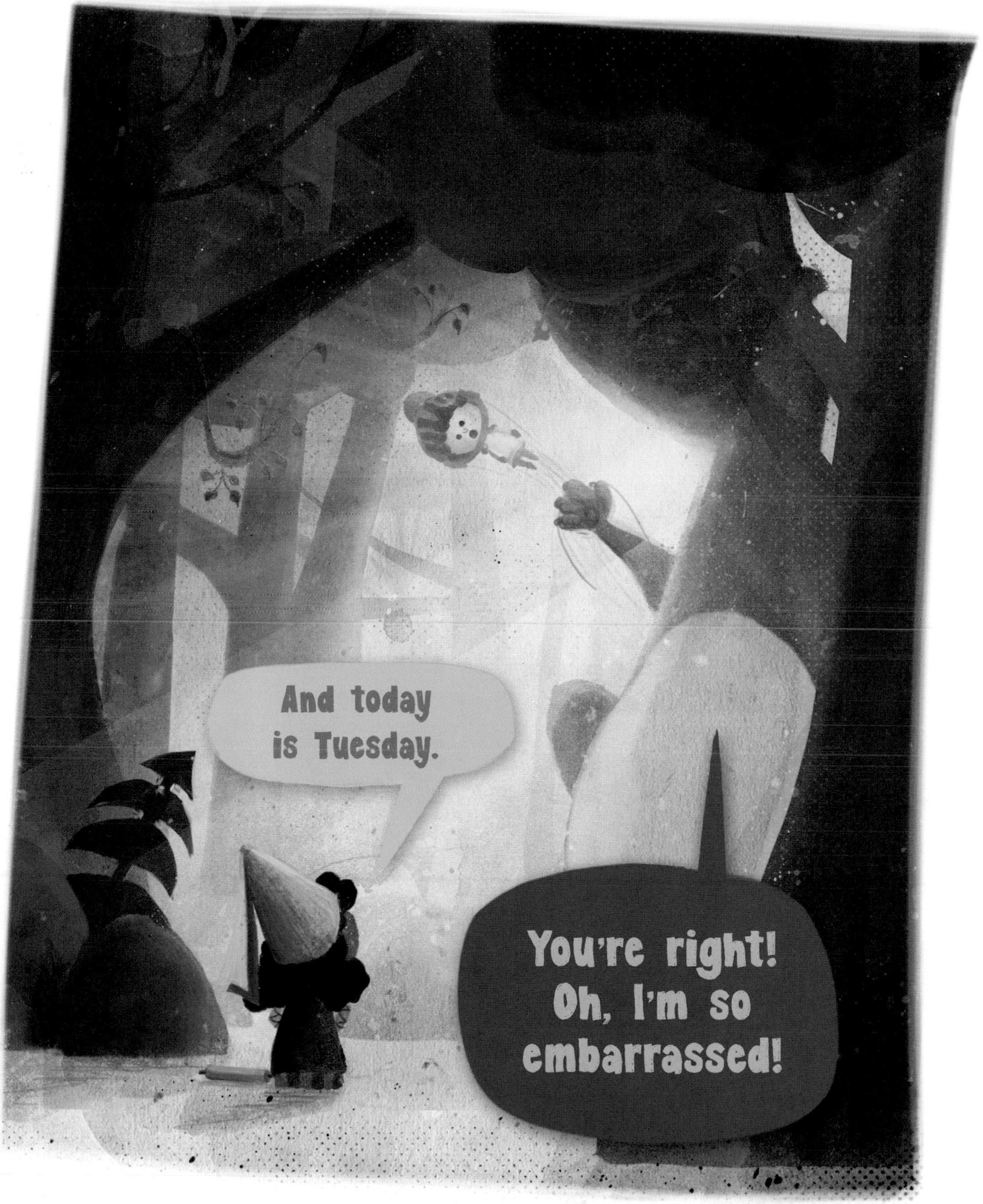
And today is Tuesday.
You're right! Oh, I'm so embarrassed!

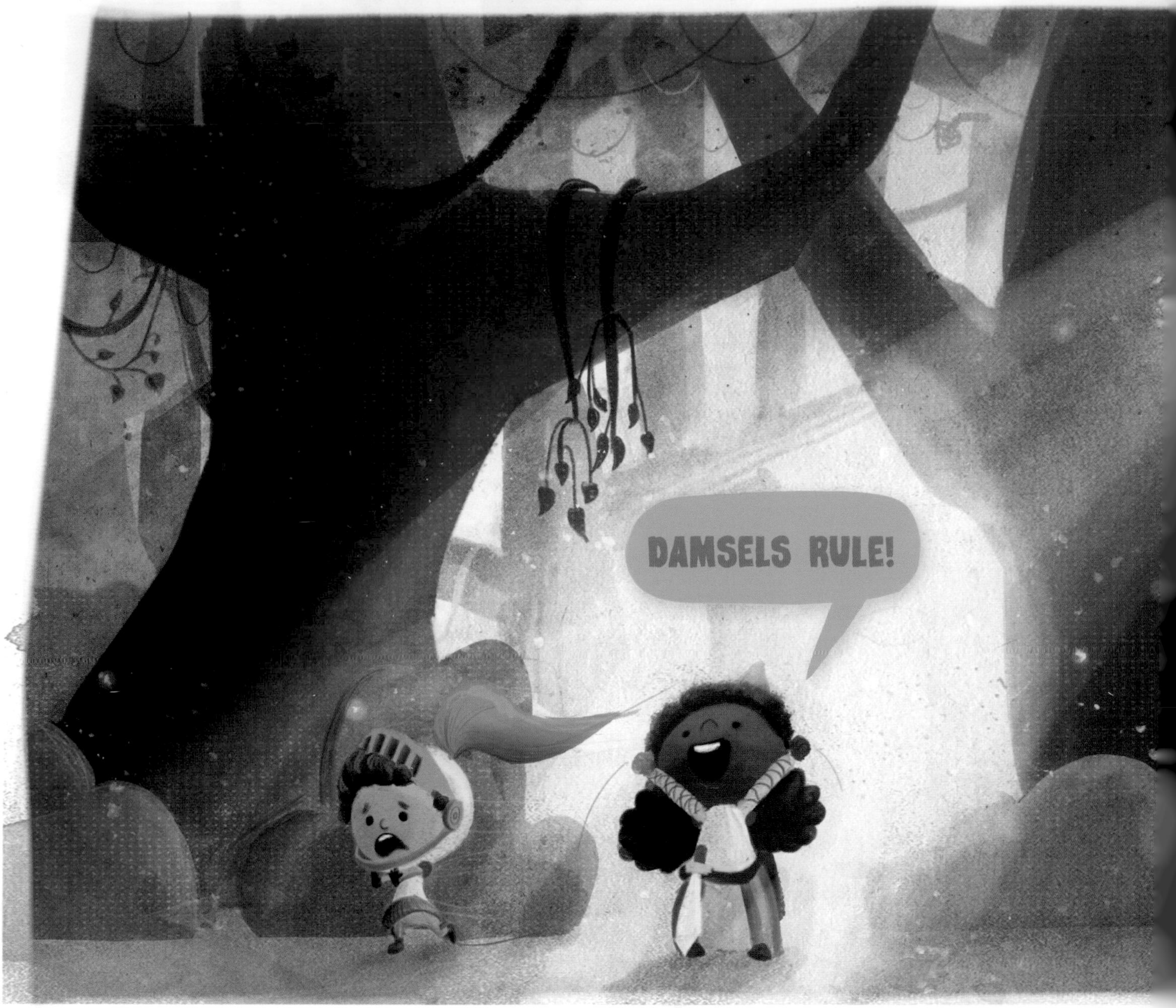
DAMSELS RULE!

That story is ridiculous. Noodles? Come on . . .
I think it's fantastic. You wanted a dragon story.
Hey, what's that?

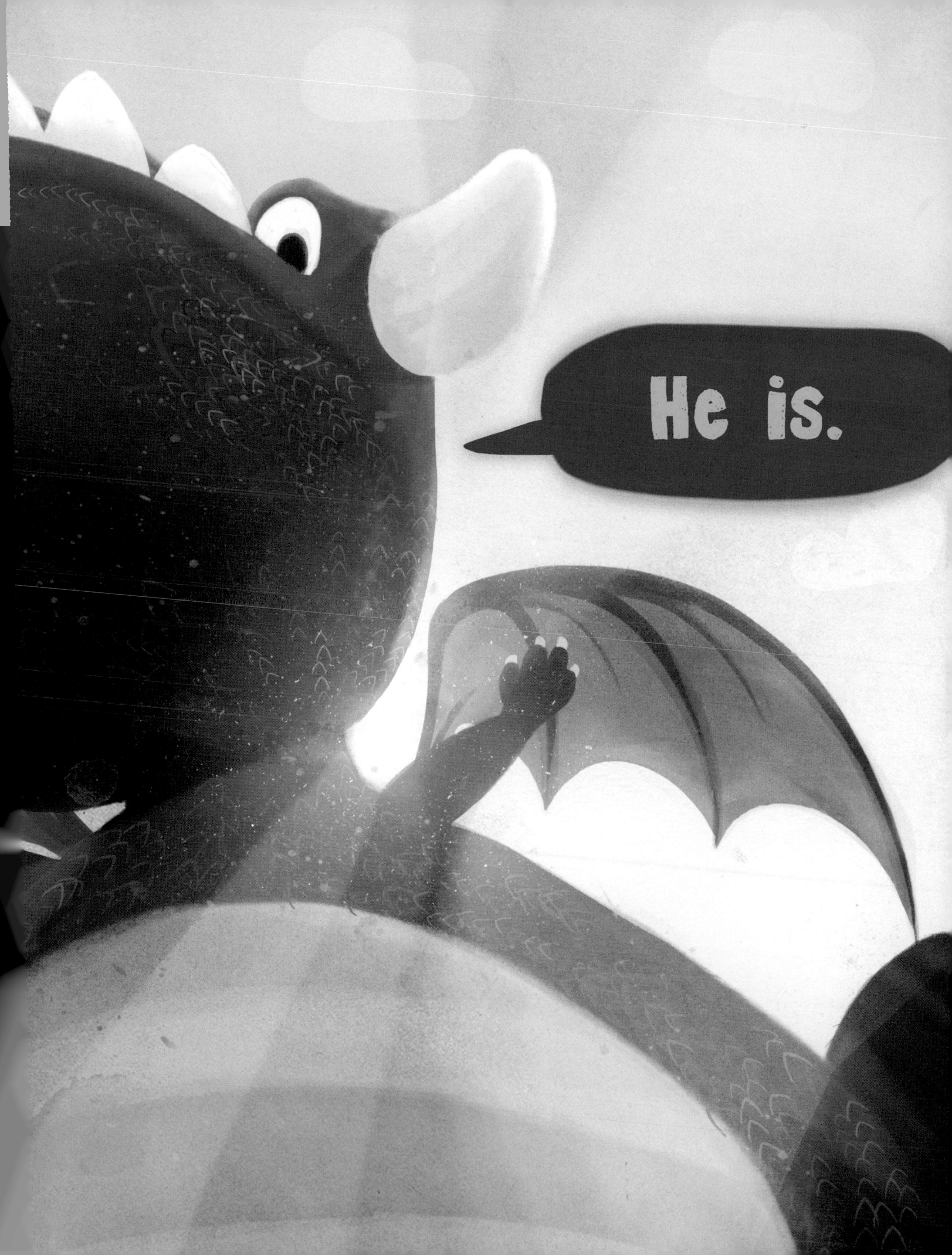
He is.

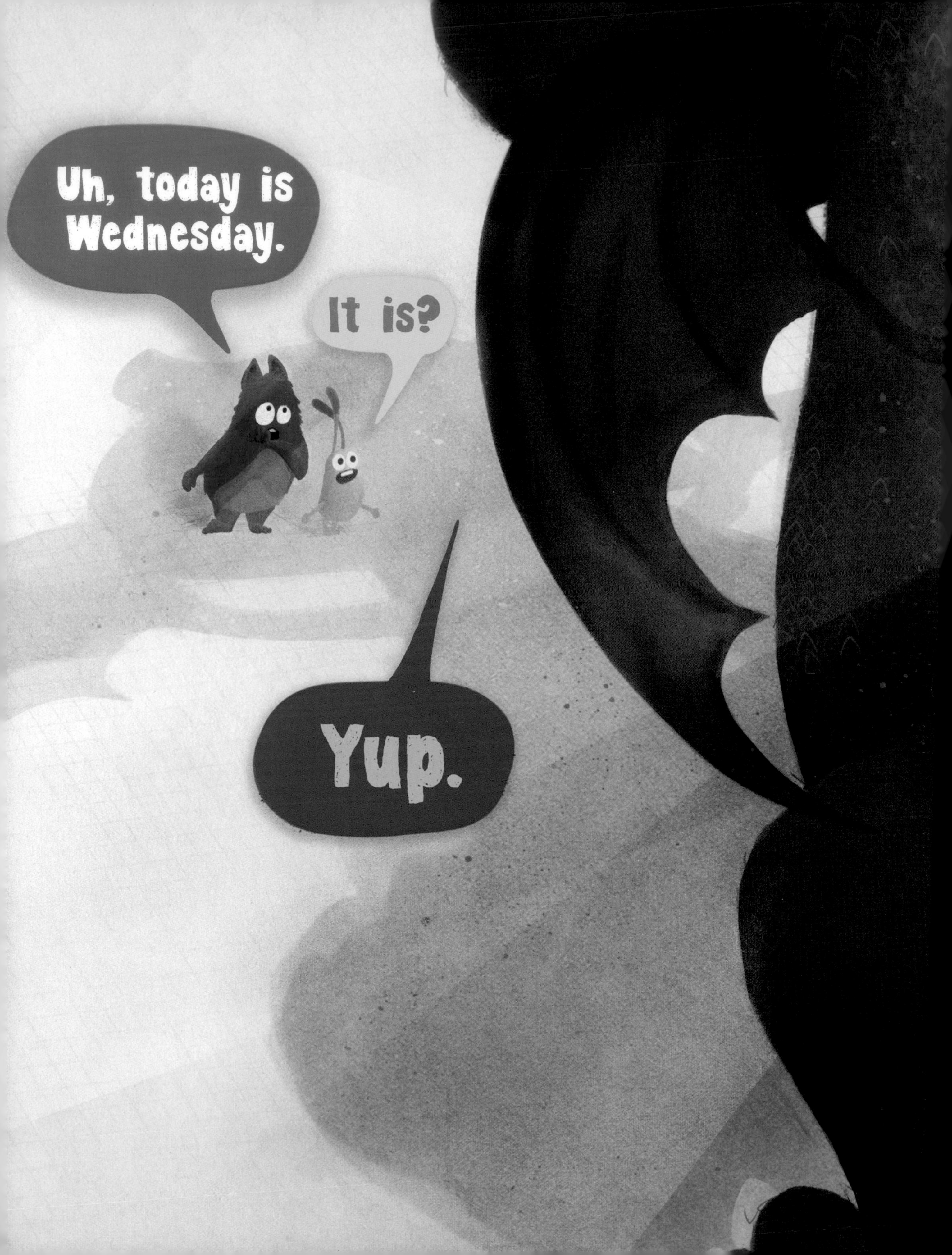
Uh, today is Wednesday.
It is?
Yup.

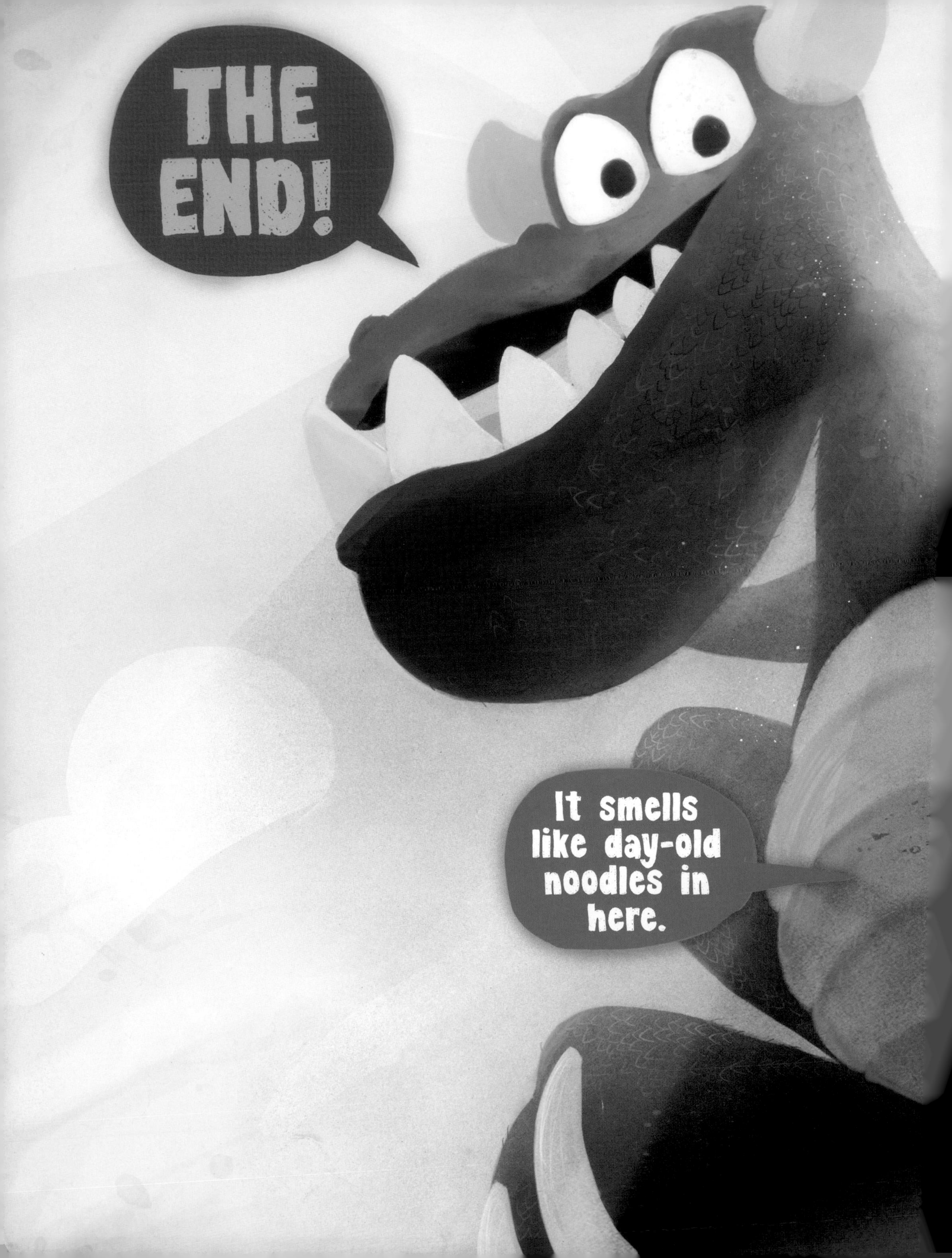
THE END!
It smells like day-old noodles in here.